JUV/E   Say, Allen.
FIC

Grandfather's
journey.

$16.45

DATE			

Grandfather's Journey

WRITTEN AND ILLUSTRATED BY

ALLEN SAY

Houghton Mifflin Company

Boston

Library of Congress Cataloging-in-Publication Data

Say, Allen.
    Grandfather's journey / Allen Say.
        p.   cm.
    Summary: A Japanese American man recounts his grandfather's
journey to America which he later also undertakes, and the feelings
of being torn by a love for two different countries.
    ISBN 0-395-57035-2
    [1. Grandfathers—Fiction.   2. Voyages and travels—Fiction.
3. Homesickness—Fiction.   4. Japan—Fiction.   5. United States—
Description and travel—Fiction.   6. Japanese Americans—Fiction.]
I. Title.
PZ7.S2744Gr   1993   93-18836
[E]—dc20   CIP
                    AC

Printed in the United States of America

HOR   10   9   8   7   6   5   4

To Richard, Francine, and Davis

My grandfather was a young man when he left his home in Japan
and went to see the world.

He wore European clothes for the first time and began his journey on
a steamship. The Pacific Ocean astonished him.

For three weeks he did not see land. When land finally appeared
it was the New World.

He explored North America by train and riverboat, and often walked for days on end.

Deserts with rocks like enormous sculptures amazed him.

The endless farm fields reminded him of the ocean he had crossed.

Huge cities of factories and tall buildings bewildered and yet excited him.

He marveled at the towering mountains and rivers as clear as the sky.

He met many people along the way. He shook hands with black men
and white men, with yellow men and red men.

The more he traveled, the more he longed to see new places, and never thought of returning home.

Of all the places he visited, he liked California best. He loved the
strong sunlight there, the Sierra Mountains, the lonely seacoast.

After a time, he returned to his village in Japan to marry his childhood sweetheart. Then he brought his bride to the new country.

They made their home by the San Francisco Bay and had a baby girl.

As his daughter grew, my grandfather began to think about his own childhood.
He thought about his old friends.

He remembered the mountains and rivers of his home. He surrounded himself with songbirds, but he could not forget.

Finally, when his daughter was nearly grown, he could wait no more.
He took his family and returned to his homeland.

Once again he saw the mountains and rivers of his childhood.
They were just as he had remembered them.

Once again he exchanged stories and laughed with his old friends.

But the village was not a place for a daughter from San Francisco.
So my grandfather bought a house in a large city nearby.

There, the young woman fell in love, married, and sometime later
I was born.

When I was a small boy, my favorite weekend was a visit to my
grandfather's house. He told me many stories about California.

He raised warblers and silvereyes, but he could not forget the mountains and rivers of California. So he planned a trip.

But a war began. Bombs fell from the sky and scattered our lives
like leaves in a storm.

When the war ended, there was nothing left of the city and of the house
where my grandparents had lived.

So they returned to the village where they had been children.
But my grandfather never kept another songbird.

The last time I saw him, my grandfather said that he longed to see California one more time. He never did.

And when I was nearly grown, I left home and went to see California
for myself.

After a time, I came to love the land my grandfather had loved, and I stayed on and on until I had a daughter of my own.

But I also miss the mountains and rivers of my childhood. I miss my old friends. So I return now and then, when I can not still the longing in my heart.

The funny thing is, the moment I am in one country,
I am homesick for the other.

I think I know my grandfather now.
I miss him very much.